P9-BYY-559

Mr. Pine's
Purple
House

BOOKS STARRING MR. PINE

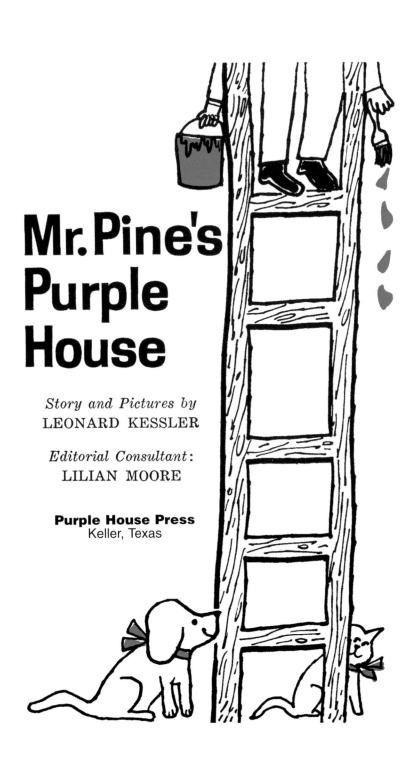

Mr. Pine's Purple House

Story and Pictures by
LEONARD KESSLER

Editorial Consultant:
LILIAN MOORE

Purple House Press
Keller, Texas

Publisher's Cataloging in Publication Data

Kessler, Leonard P.
Mr. Pine's purple house / story and pictures by Leonard Kessler; [edited by] Lilian Moore
p. cm.
SUMMARY: Mr. Pine lives in a little white house on Vine Street, where there
are FIFTY white houses all in a line. How can Mr. Pine tell which one is his?
ISBN 1-930900-02-3
[1. Colors - Fiction.   2. People - Fiction.]
I. Moore, Lilian.   II. Title.
PZ7.K484 M57 2000
[Fic] - dc21 00-104411

Purple House Press and turtle logo
are trademarks of Purple House Press, Ltd. Co.

Purple House Press
Keller, TX 76248
Visit us on the Internet at www.PurpleHousePress.com

Printed in Malaysia by Tien Wah Press
1 2 3 4 5 6 7 8 9 10
First Edition

MEET MR. PINE

Some of the questions that readers
ask are, "Do you look like Mr. Pine?"
and "Are you really Mr. Pine?"

Well yes and no.

Mr. Pine wears glasses.
I also wear glasses.
Mr. Pine has a dog and a cat.
We had a dog named Spanky,
and a black cat named Bianca.
Mr. Pine had a mustache,
but I have never grown a mustache.
Mr. Pine loves to wear hats.
I love to wear hats too,
especially baseball caps.
Recently I opened a package from
the GAP and my wife Ethel said,
"Oh, NO!" Not another HAT!"

Mr. Pine paints signs and houses.
When I was a senior in high school
I worked part-time as a sign painter
at the Pennywise Supermarket
in Pittsburgh, Pennsylvania.

"Am I really Mr. Pine?"

Our very first house in Rockland
County, New York was painted
light PURPLE!

INTRODUCTION

These books are meant to help the young reader discover what a delightful experience reading can be. The stories are such fun that they urge the child to try new reading skills. They are so easy to read that they will encourage and strengthen the child as a reader.

The adult will notice that the sentences aren't too long, the words aren't too hard, and the skillful repetition is like a helping hand. What the child will feel is: "This is a good story – and I can read it myself!"

For some children, the best way to meet these stories may be to hear them read aloud at first. Others, who are better prepared to read on their own, may need a little help in the beginning – help that is best given freely. Youngsters who have more experience in reading alone – whether in first or second or third grade – will have the immediate joy of reading "all by myself."

These books have been planned to help all young readers grow – in their pleasure in books and in their power to read them.

Lilian Moore
Specialist in Reading
Formerly of Division of Instructional Research,
New York City Board of Education

Mr. Pine lived

on Vine Street

in a little white house.

"A white house is fine,"
said Mr. Pine,
"but there are
FIFTY white houses
all in a line
on Vine Street.
How can I tell
which one
is mine?"

He looked up and down
the street.

"I know,"
said Mr. Pine.
"I will plant a tree,
a little pine tree,
by my house.

Pine tree.
Pine's house.
See?
That's me!"

"That's what I will do," he said.

And that is what he did.

Mr. Gold lived
next door to Mr. Pine.
"What a nice little tree!"
said Mr. Gold.

Mrs. Green lived
next door to Mr. Gold.
"What a pretty tree!"
said Mrs. Green.

13

Mrs. Brown lived
next door to Mrs. Green.
"What a very nice tree!"
said Mrs. Brown.

The next day
Mr. Pine looked
out of his window.
He wanted to see
his little pine tree.

But what did he see?

He saw

fifty white houses

all in a line.

And there was

a little pine tree

by each house.

"OH, NO!"

said Mr. Pine.

"Now, how can I tell
which house is mine!"

He looked up and down
the street again.

"I know,"

said Mr. Pine.

"I will plant

a big bush

next to

the little pine tree."

"Hmmmmmm.

Big bush.

Pine tree.

Pine's house.

See?

That's me!"

And he did!

Then he did this:

and this:

"There!"

said Mr. Pine.

"That looks just fine."

"What a pretty bush!"
said Mr. Gold.

"Oh, how nice!"
said Mrs. Green.

"Very, VERY pretty!"
said Mrs. Brown.

The next morning
Mr. Pine looked
out of his window.
He wanted to see
his big bush
by his little pine tree.

But what did he see?

There were

fifty white houses

all in a line.

There were

fifty little green trees,

all of them pine.

And next to each tree

there was a big bush.

"OH, NO!"

said Mr. Pine.

"OH, NO!"

All the houses

still looked the same.

Mr. Pine thought and thought.

"I know,"

said Mr. Pine.

"I will paint my house."

He thought and thought
some more.

"Let me see," he said.

"Red? Yellow? Orange?

No.

Blue? Green? Pink?

Let me see.

I know.

I will paint my house . . .

PURPLE!"

Then off he went

to get the paint.

"I want to buy
some paint,"
said Mr. Pine to Mr. Dash.

"I want to paint
my house purple."

"Purple?"
asked Mr. Dash.

"Yes, purple,"
said Mr. Pine.

"Green is very nice," said Mr. Dash.

"NO," said Mr. Pine.

"Red is very nice," said Mr. Dash.

"NO," said Mr. Pine.

"White is very very nice,"

"No, no, NO!"

said Mr. Pine.

"I want purple paint!"

"Purple paint!"
said Mr. Dash.
"Think of that!
Well, for your house
you will need
nine big cans
of purple paint."

"I will need
some brushes, too,"
said Mr. Pine.

"And this:

and this:

Then I need something
to mix the paint
and to clean
the brushes."

Mr. Pine put everything

into his truck.

Back he went to Vine Street.

He put
his tall ladder
here.

He put
his little ladder
here.

"I have things
to do before I paint,"
said Mr. Pine.
"Mix and fix,

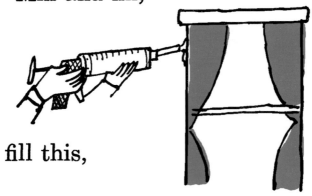

fill this,

and sweep this."

"Mix, mix, mix.

Now the paint

is just right.

Now

I can paint!"

Then Mr. Pine went up the ladder
to the very top of the house.

He began to paint.

Squish, squish

went the brush.

Squish, squish, squish.

Some boys
were playing ball
in the street.
But Mr. Pine
did not see them.

A boy hit the ball.

Up went the ball.

Up,

up, up.

It was a home run.

"Look out,

Mr. Pine!

Look out!"

the boys called.

But Mr. Pine

did not hear them.

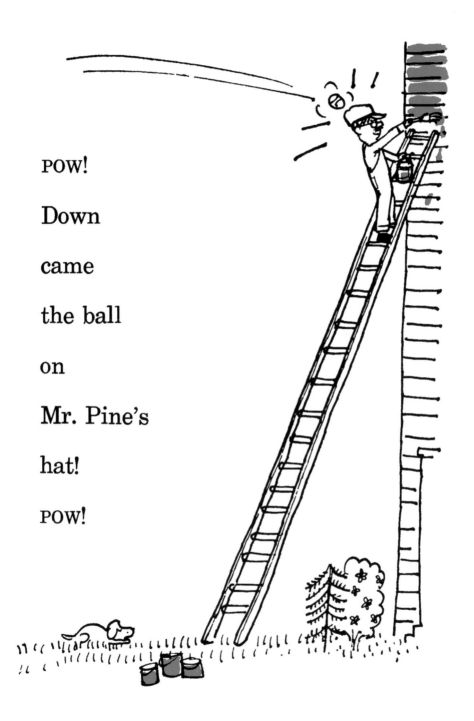

POW!

Down

came

the ball

on

Mr. Pine's

hat!

POW!

Down came
the brushes.
Down came
the purple paint.
Down came
Mr. Pine!

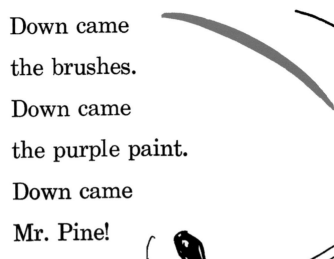

"Now I have to get more paint,"
said Mr. Pine.

He went up the ladder again.

Squish, squish
went his brush.
Squish, squish, squish.

Then Mrs. Gold's cat
ran under the ladder.
Mr. Pine's dog
ran after
the little cat.
Round and round
they ran.
Grrrrrrrrrrr!
Meoww, meoww!
Grrrrrrrrrrrrrr!
Mewwwwwwwwwwwwww!

The little cat
ran up the ladder.
But Mr. Pine did not see her.
Mr. Pine came
down the ladder,
down on the
little cat's foot.

MEOOOOOOOOOOOOOOW!

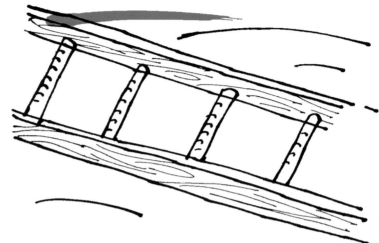

Down came the cat.

Down came the brushes.

Down came the ladder.

Down came the paint.

Down

came

Mr. Pine.

POW!

Now Mr. Pine had

purple grass,

a purple cat,

a purple dog,

a purple hat,

and a purple nose.

"Now I have to get
more purple paint,"
said Mr. Pine.
Up the ladder
he went again.

Squish, squish.

Mr. Pine painted

and painted

until the house

was all purple.

Everybody on Vine Street

came to look

at Mr. Pine's

purple house.

No one had seen

a purple house before.

"What a nice purple!"

said Mrs. Gray.

"I will paint MY house!"

"What a pretty purple house!"

said Mr. Gold.

"I will paint MY house!"

"What a very pretty

purple house!"

said Mrs. Green.

"I will paint my house, too!"

"OH, NO! NO! NO!"
said Mr. Pine.

"Not FIFTY PURPLE HOUSES,
all in a line
on Vine Street!"

"But I will paint
my house pink,"
said Mrs. Gray.

"Yellow for me,"
said Mrs. Green.

"Green for me,"
said Mrs. Brown.

"I like red,"
Mrs. White said.

"And I will keep my house
all white," said Mr. Gold.

Now there are

fifty houses on Vine Street.

There are red houses,

and green houses,

and brown houses.

There are yellow and pink houses,

and there are

some white houses, too.

But there is

just one

purple house

on Vine Street . . . .

And that is Mr. Pine's purple house!